PUFFIN BOOKS

BAD KITTY
GETS A BATH

Nick Bruel is the author and illustrator of the bestselling Bad Kitty series. He is also a freelance cartoonist and illustrator and lives with his wife and daughter in New York.

Books by Nick Bruel

BAD KITTY GETS A BATH

BAD KITTY

GETS A BATH

NICK BRUEL

PUFFIN

For Jules, Jenny, Kate, Halley, Julie
and the rest of the fabulous Feiffers

PUFFIN BOOKS

Published by the Penguin Group
Penguin Books Ltd, 80 Strand, London WC2R 0RL, England
Penguin Group (USA) Inc., 375 Hudson Street, New York, New York 10014, USA
Penguin Group (Canada), 90 Eglinton Avenue East, Suite 700, Toronto, Ontario, Canada M4P 2Y3
(a division of Pearson Penguin Canada Inc.)
Penguin Ireland, 25 St Stephen's Green, Dublin 2, Ireland (a division of Penguin Books Ltd)
Penguin Group (Australia), 250 Camberwell Road, Camberwell, Victoria 3124, Australia
(a division of Pearson Australia Group Pty Ltd)
Penguin Books India Pvt Ltd, 11 Community Centre, Panchsheel Park, New Delhi – 110 017, India
Penguin Group (NZ), 67 Apollo Drive, Rosedale, North Shore 0632, New Zealand
(a division of Pearson New Zealand Ltd)
Penguin Books (South Africa) (Pty) Ltd, 24 Sturdee Avenue, Rosebank,
Johannesburg 2196, South Africa

Penguin Books Ltd, Registered Offices: 80 Strand, London WC2R 0RL, England

puffinbooks.com

First published in the USA by Square Fish, an imprint of Macmillan, 2008
Published in Great Britain in Puffin Books 2011

ISBN: 978-0-141-33593-3

www.greenpenguin.co.uk

Penguin Books is committed to a sustainable future
for our business, our readers and our planet.
The book in your hands is made from paper
certified by the Forest Stewardship Council.

• CONTENTS •

As you read this book, you'll notice that there's an *
following some of the words.

Those words are defined in the Glossary*
at the back of this book.

• INTRODUCTION •

This is how Kitty likes to clean herself.

SHE LICKS
HERSELF.

She licks her leg.

She licks her tail.

She licks her back.

And to clean her face, she licks her front paw and rubs it all over where her tongue can't reach.

3

LICK LICK LICK
LICK LICK LICK
LICK LICK LICK
LICK LICK LICK
LICK LICK LICK
LICK LICK LICK
LICK LICK LICK
LICK LICK LICK
LICK LICK LICK
LICK LICK LICK
LICK LICK LICK

Sometimes, Kitty will do this for hours.

This is a close-up of Kitty's tongue. It is covered with hundreds of tiny fish-hook-shaped barbs called "papillae".* These barbs help her to comb her fur as she licks herself. Her tongue also collects any loose fur that she could swallow.

Papillae are partly made of fibrous protein called keratin. Do you know what else is made of keratin? *Your fingernails!*

HOLY SALAMI! THAT *GOOFY* CAT'S GOT HUNDREDS OF TINY FINGERNAILS ON HER TONGUE!

Kitty has to be careful.
Sometimes, if she
licks her fur too much,
she can develop a
HAIR BALL.

Hair balls
form in Kitty's
stomach when
she swallows
too much fur.

Sometimes, the
only way to get
rid of a hair ball
is to cough it up.

GNNNNn...

Coughing up
a hair ball isn't
always easy.

They can be
stubborn.

HACK

And sometimes
those hair balls
can be pretty
darn big.

WARNING!

You should NEVER clean yourself
the same way as Kitty!

DAILY NOOZ

KID SENT HOME FOR BAD BREATH—ALL OVER BODY

SCHOOL EVACUATED

"I forgot that I ate a garlic and egg pizza for lunch," said the boy, seen here in this picture walking home and wishing to remain anonymous.

"Well, I saw my cat cleaning herself with her tongue," said the child. "So I thought to myself, 'Gee, that looks like it could work on me, too!'"

Officials predict that the school will be re-opened in about a week, once health officials have dealt with

"We tried soaking the child in a solution made of toothpaste and mouthwash," said Principal Sarah Bellum. "But it just helped a little. We can only hope that this incident serves as a warning to

So, this is how Kitty *USUALLY* cleans herself.

LICK

LICK

LICK

LICK

LICKETY-
LICK

BUT . . .

Sometimes . . .

every now and then . . .

Kitty needs . . .

a real . . .

19

• CHAPTER ONE •

PREPARING KITTY'S BATH

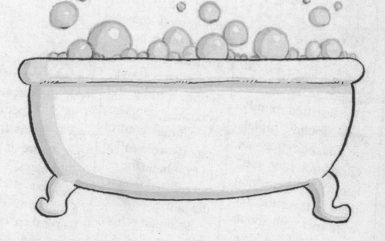

Do you remember the last time you tried to give Kitty a bath?

DAILY NOOZ

ENTIRE FAMILY FLEES FOR LIFE

The grisly story began when a local family, unprepared for giving their beloved cat a bath, was forced to evacuate their house after the kitty went on a screaming, biting, spitting and scratching rampage.

The terrified family was found hiding in this oak tree six kilometres from their home. All pleas asking them to leave the tree were met with shouts of "Eek", "Yipes" and "This is worse than when we ran out of food for the kitty."

Animal control experts were called in to subdue the cat but refused to enter the house.

Said one officer, "We see this sort of thing every time someone tries to give a cat a bath."

"Oh, the screams! I shall remember the screams from that house in my nightmares," said neighbour Mrs Edna Kroninger. "It was worse than the day they ran out of food for the kitty. I almost moved out of the neighbourhood that day."

BE PREPARED.

The first lesson that all cat owners must learn is that . . .

CATS HATE BATHS

For your own safety, please repeat this to yourself four thousand eight hundred and ninety-three times.

It's not that cats don't *like* baths. It's not that cats have a difficult relationship with baths. It's not that cats chose not to vote for baths in the last election. It's not that cats would rather choose vanilla over baths. It's not that cats neglect to send baths a card on their birthdays. It's not that cats pick baths last when choosing sides for a kick ball game. It's not that cats think about baths in the same way a fire hydrant thinks about dogs. It's not that cats look at baths in the same way that a vegetarian looks at five kilos of raw liver. It's not that cats once bought baths an awesome present that cost an entire month's pocket money, and then baths didn't even have the decency to say "thank you".

It's simply that . . .

Think about it this way . . .

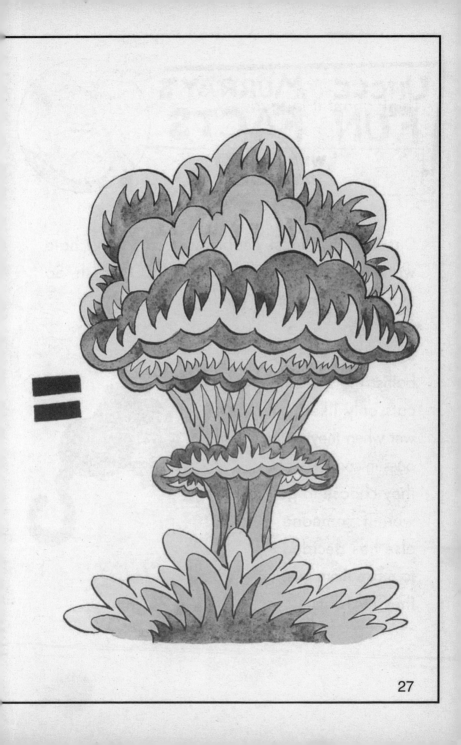

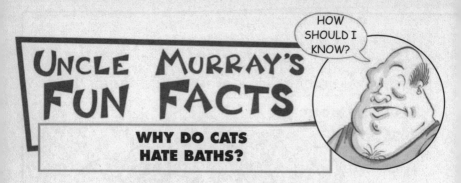

UNCLE MURRAY'S FUN FACTS

WHY DO CATS HATE BATHS?

Despite what most people say, cats don't hate water. Fish live in water, and cats LOVE fish. So most cats don't mind getting a little wet.

But cats do HATE baths. That's because cats only like to get wet when they're the ones in control, when they choose to get wet. If someone else has decided to make them wet, they HATE it.

And if a cat *has* to get wet, the water had better be warm.

A cat's fur is very good at keeping her warm, but not so good at keeping her dry. So if a cat gets wet in cold weather, that poor cat will have a hard time getting warm again. And that poor cat could catch a bad cold.

So, cats should always be bathed in warm (NOT HOT) water.

ME, I LIKE TO SHOWER IN THE MORNING WHILE I SING OLD SHOW TUNES LIKE "SOMEWHERE OVER THE RAINBOW"!

Cats hate showers, too. And they rarely sing old show tunes.

Now that you understand that cats hate baths (you will be tested), you will find it much easier to prepare Kitty's bath BEFORE putting her in it.

The following are some of the items you will need for Kitty's bath:

ONE BATHTUB

PLENTY OF WARM WATER

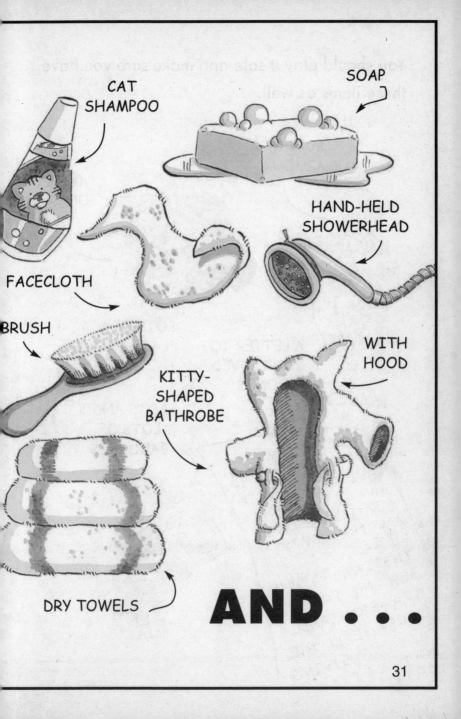

CAT SHAMPOO

SOAP

HAND-HELD SHOWERHEAD

FACECLOTH

BRUSH

WITH HOOD

KITTY-SHAPED BATHROBE

DRY TOWELS

AND . . .

You should play it safe and make sure you have these items as well.

SUIT OF ARMOUR

YOUR DOCTOR ON SPEED DIAL

A LETTER TO YOUR LOVED ONES

LOTS OF PLASMA*

LOTS AND LOTS OF BANDAGES

DEAR FAMILY,
I AM GOING TO GIVE KITTY A BATH. DO NOT CRY FOR ME. I HAVE LIVED A LONG, HAPPY LIFE.

INSTEAD, REMEMBER ME FOR MY BRAVERY AND COURAGE IN THE FACE OF GIVING THAT CAT A BATH

CLEAN UNDERWEAR (BECAUSE STRESSFUL SITUATIONS CAN CAUSE "ACCIDENTS")

PLANE TICKETS AND A MAP TO YOUR AUNT PAULINE'S HOUSE WHERE YOU CAN HIDE WHEN THIS IS OVER

A SCRATCHING POST MADE TO LOOK LIKE YOU THAT MIGHT (BUT PROBABLY WON'T) FOOL KITTY

AN AMBULANCE IN YOUR DRIVEWAY WITH THE ENGINE RUNNING

And, of course, the last thing you'll need before giving Kitty a bath will be Kitty herself.

But try not to say that out loud.

QUICK QUIZ

FILL IN THE BLANK.

CATS *Hate baths*

A) LOVE BATHS.

B) LIKE BATHS.

C) HATE BATHS.

D) ARE SMALL, FLIGHTLESS, DOMESTIC FOWL EASILY RECOGNIZED BY THEIR COMBS AND WATTLES* THAT CAN LAY AS MANY AS 250 EGGS A YEAR.

ANSWER: The correct answer is C. If you answered anything other than C, please reread Chapter One 753 more times or until you are saying "Cats Hate Baths" out loud in your sleep. If you answered D, please go immediately to an optician, because the animal in your home that you think is a cat is really a chicken.

36

• CHAPTER TWO •

FINDING KITTY

Now comes the hard part.

The bath is ready, but Kitty is not. In fact, Kitty is nowhere to be found.

Is she in her litter tray?

NOPE.

Is she under the sofa?

NOPE.

Is she sitting
on her favourite
window ledge?

NOPE.

Is she sitting in
her favourite
chair?

NOPE.

Is she lying
in your bed?

NOPE.

So where is
Kitty?

Kitty's very good at hiding. So maybe the best step right now would be to think about where you found her all the other times she hid.

This is where she was hiding when you had to take her to the vet.*

This is where she was hiding when you had to brush her teeth.

This is where she
was hiding when
you had to give
her medicine.

This is where she was
hiding when you had to
clip her nails.

This is where she
was hiding when
you told her
to finish her
vegetables.*

There's Puppy!

Maybe Puppy knows where Kitty is hiding.

Hey, Puppy . . . Do you know where Kitty is hiding?

Hmmm . . . Maybe he doesn't know.

Hold on . . . Since when does Puppy have black fur? Puppy has never had black fur. So maybe that isn't Puppy at all. So who is it really? Hmmm . . .

44

IT'S KITTY IN DISGUISE!

GET HER!

SHE'S RUNNING INTO THE LIVING ROOM!

GET HER!

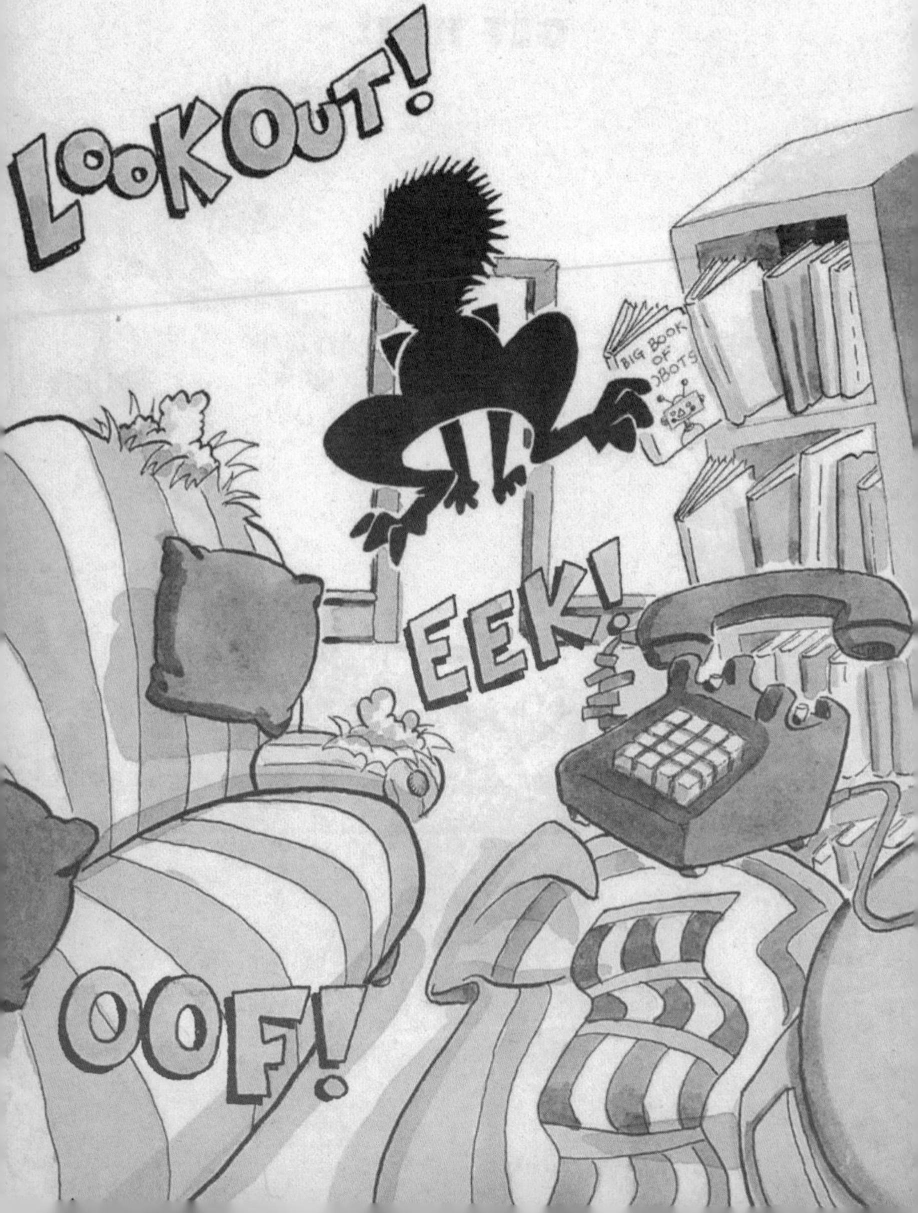

SHE'S RUNNING UPSTAIRS!
GET HER!

SHE'S IN THE BATHROOM! She's trapped. Now, all we have to do is calmly close the door, and we can begin her bath.

• CHAPTER THREE •

HOW TO
GIVE KITTY
A BATH

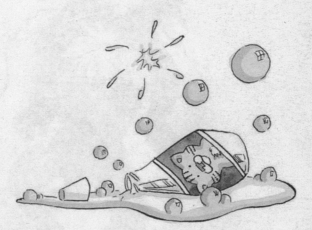

Now that you have Kitty, and the bath is prepared, please follow these simple steps carefully so that both you and she are comfortable during the bath.

1) Gently but firmly gather Kitty up in your arms.

2) Pet her and caress her lovingly to reassure Kitty that all is well.

3) Tell Kitty that you love her. No doubt Kitty will tell you that she loves you, too.

I LOVE
YOU, TOO!

4) Now, gently lower Kitty into the warm, soapy water for her bath.

OH MY!
THIS ISN'T
SO BAD!

I HAVE WRONGED YOU! AND TO MAKE UP FOR MY WRETCHED BEHAVIOUR, I SHALL REWARD YOU . . .

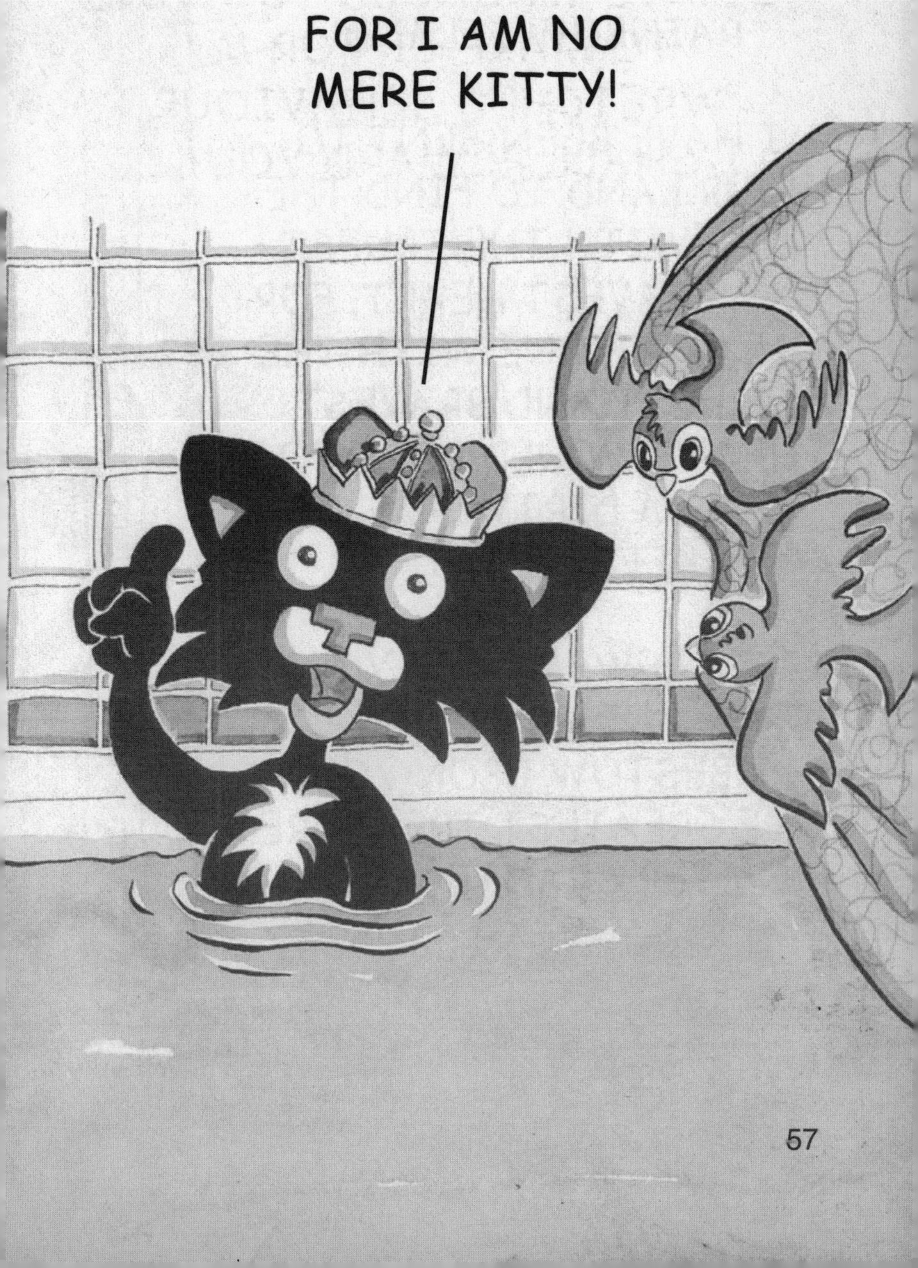
FOR I AM NO
MERE KITTY!

I AM QUEEN ESMERELDA,*
KITTY OF MAGIC CANDY
RAINBOW ISLAND!

I HAVE BEEN SENT TO
YOUR LAND TO FIND THE
ONE WITH THE TRUEST
AND BRAVEST HEART, FOR
ONLY THE ONE WITH THE
TRUEST AND BRAVEST
HEART WOULD DARE TO
GIVE A DIRTY, SMELLY
KITTY A BATH!

AS A REWARD FOR YOUR
TRUE AND BRAVE HEART,
I BESTOW UPON YOU
THE GREATEST TREASURE
EVER GRANTED . . .

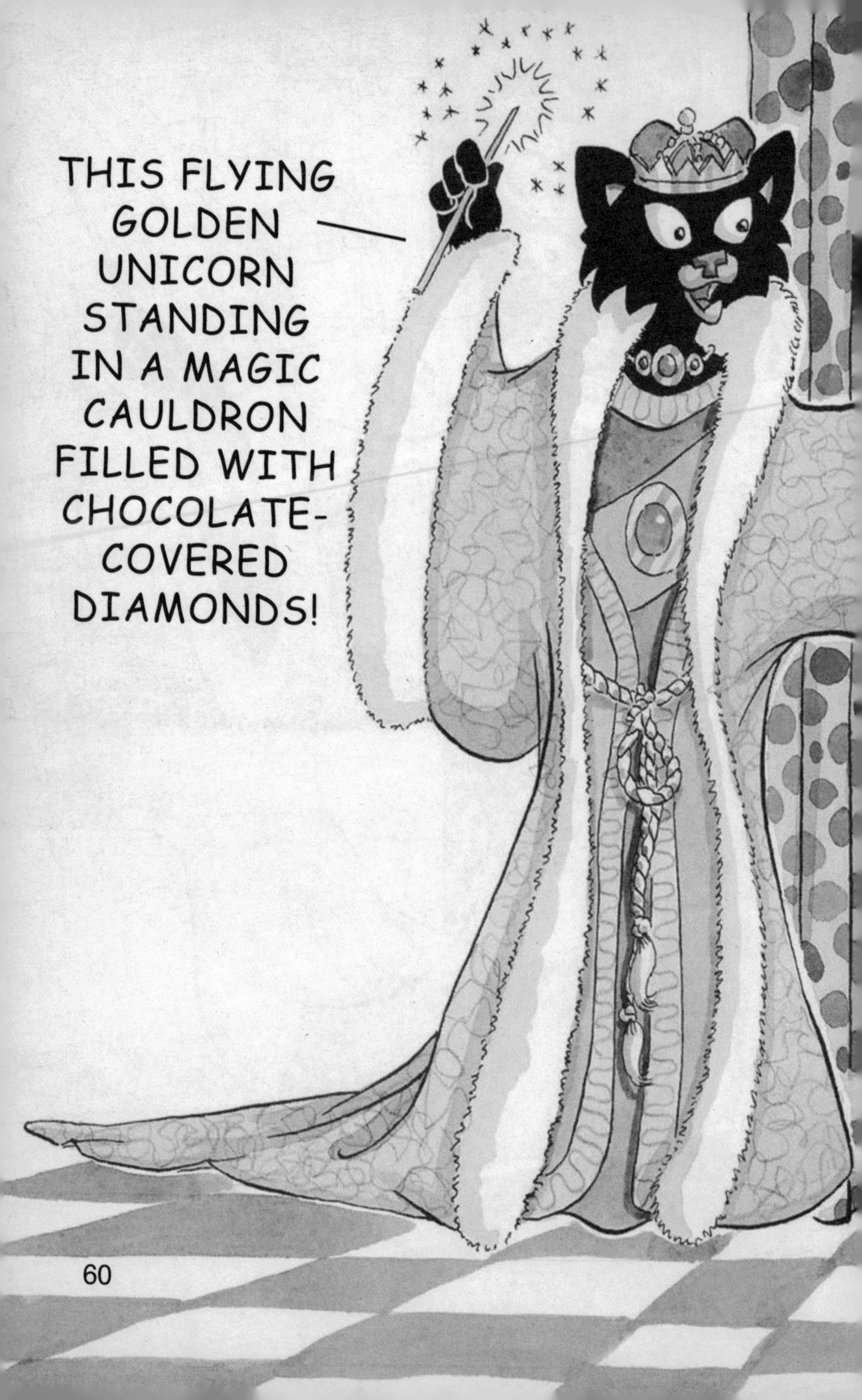

THIS FLYING
GOLDEN —
UNICORN
STANDING
IN A MAGIC
CAULDRON
FILLED WITH
CHOCOLATE-
COVERED
DIAMONDS!

We regret to
inform you that
Chapter Three
was a dream.

• CHAPTER FOUR •

GETTING KITTY INTO THE WATER

You must have known it would be harder than that.

Now that you've regained consciousness, you probably remember what happened when . . .

You took her to the vet.

You made her
brush her
teeth.

You made her take
her medicine.

You clipped her nails.

You made her
finish her
vegetables.

Nick,
I'm sorry, but this image is much too
gruesome and violent for us to publish
in this book. If we were to show what
Kitty did here, we would give the
*readers nightmares for at least**
fifty years.

*Your editor,**
Neal

Well, none of that matters now, because Kitty . . . YOU STINK! And you NEED TO TAKE A BATH.

Tell Kitty in a firm voice that she needs to get into that bathtub NOW!

Okay. That didn't work.

You might want to try the subtle art of NEGOTIATION.*

Negotiation is a way of using words instead of force to try and convince Kitty to do something she doesn't want to do.

69

First, try FLATTERY.

LOOK AT THE PRETTY KITTY!
SUCH A SWEET, WONDERFUL,
PRETTY KITTY! DOESN'T THE
PRETTY, PRETTY KITTY WANT
TO BE ALL NICE AND CLEAN
AND SMELL JUST LIKE A
BEAUTIFUL FLOWER? WHAT
A PRETTY KITTY! WHO IS
THE PRETTIEST KITTY IN THE
WHOLE WIDE WORLD?
YOU ARE! YES, YOU ARE!
YOU PRETTY, PRETTY,
SWEET LITTLE KITTY, YOU!

If that doesn't work, try . . .

BEGGING.

PLEASE! PLEEEEASE!
PLEASE GET IN THE BATHTUB!
PLEEEASE!
IF THERE IS EVEN A SCRAP
OF GOODNESS IN YOU,
WON'T YOU PLEEEASE
GET IN THE BATHTUB?
PLEEEASE!
I'VE WORKED SO HARD TO GET
YOU HERE AND NOW YOU'RE
ALMOST IN THE TUB! YOU'RE
SO CLOSE! WON'T YOU
PLEEEASE GET IN THE TUB?
PLEEEEEEEEASE!

I'LL BE YOUR BEST FRIEND.

If that doesn't work, try . . .

BRIBERY.

OH, KITTY . . . YOU KNOW
THAT FANCY SCRATCHING
POST MADE OUT OF SILK AND
RHINOCEROS HIDE YOU LIKE?
WELL, I'LL BUY IT FOR YOU IF
YOU GET IN THE TUB. AND
YOU LIKE THOSE GOAT TAIL
AND SALMON FIN TREATS,
DON'T YOU? I'LL BUY YOU THE
BIGGEST BOX IN THE STORE
IF YOU GET IN THE TUB. DID I
SAY "BOX"? I MEANT "BARREL"!
DID I SAY "BARREL"? I MEANT
"TRUCKLOAD"! AND YOU CAN
EAT THEM WHILE YOU TAKE
YOUR BATH. DO WE HAVE A
DEAL, KITTY?

KITTY?

If that doesn't work, try . . .

REVERSE PSYCHOLOGY.*

OKAY . . . IF YOU DON'T WANT
TO TAKE A BATH . . . FINE!
DON'T TAKE A BATH. SEE IF I
CARE. YOU'LL SMELL TERRIBLE
FOR THE REST OF YOUR LIFE
AND NO ONE WILL LIKE
BEING NEAR YOU, BUT THAT'S
OKAY BY ME. WHATEVER YOU
DO, DON'T GET INTO THAT
BATHTUB. THAT'S THE ONLY
WAY YOU'LL GET CLEAN, AND
WE WOULDN'T WANT THAT.
I'M HAPPY YOU'RE NOT GOING
TO TAKE A BATH. I REALLY
AM. I HOPE YOU NEVER, EVER
TAKE A BATH . . . UNLESS . . .

YOU REALLY WANT TO.

DO YOU?

Oh, well . . . It looks like Kitty is not going to be taking a bath after all. Sorry. We really tried, though.

Maybe we should just end the book right now and save some paper.

It really is too bad, because the only way we'll be able to give *Puppy* a bath is if Kitty goes first.

Didn't you know that, Kitty? Puppy is even dirt-
ier and smellier than you. He's going to need
an EXTRA-SPECIAL BATH . . .

and lots
and lots of
soap . . .

and lots
and lots of
scrubbing!

TOILET
BRUSH

PAINTBRUSH

TOOTHBRUSH

CHIMNEY
BRUSH

AIEEE! MERCY!

SNICKER

But, of course, that's never going to happen if Kitty doesn't take her bath first.

Well, I'll be . . .

• CHAPTER FIVE •

THE
BATH

Now that you finally have Kitty in the bathtub, gently use a cup or small pot to pour warm bathwater over her to soak her fur.

Try not to pour water directly on to Kitty's head. Instead, use a soft, moist cloth and gently wipe her face and head.

Use a cat shampoo recommended by Kitty's vet to clean her dirty fur.

...ay have noticed that Kitty's been making ...f noise. She's probably trying to tell you ...ing. The following is a list of common cat ... and their meanings.

MEOW ⟶ I am hungry.

MEEE
OOO ⟶ I am very hungry.
WWW?

MEE   I'm pretty darn
OOW   hungry, and you'd
RRR ⟶ better feed me
OWW right now or suffer
RRR!   the horrible
     consequences.

Rinse Kitty off using a hand-held shower attachment if you have one. If not, gently pour water over her as you did earlier.

HISSS!

Again, try not to soak Kitty's head, and use that facecloth to wipe excess soap and water from her face.

Keep rinsing and soaking and you're absolutely certain you' the shampoo.

You a lot some soun

FFT!
FFT!
FFT!

MEO

FFT! ⟶ I want to be alone.

HISSS! ⟶ Back off, pal!

MEOWR
REOWR ⟶ Unless you're really tired of living, please understand that I am in a very bad mood.
FFT!

MEOWR
REOWR
YEOWR
HISS
FFT ⟶
FFT
FFT
MEOWR!

Nick,
Sorry, but once again we can't print this. What Kitty says is so horrible and repulsive that we could all go to jail for the rest of our lives if this was printed.

Hope you understand.
Your editor,
Neal

You now have a very, very clean Kitty, even though she is also a very, very wet Kitty.

Gently remove her from the bathtub and drain the bathwater.

Dry Kitty off by wrapping her in a clean towel and rubbing her all over.

And Kitty will be nice
and dry!

What a clean, sweet-
smelling Kitty!

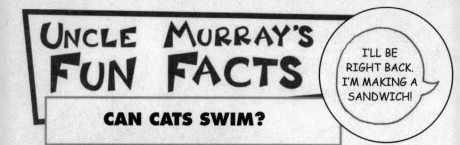

UNCLE MURRAY'S FUN FACTS

CAN CATS SWIM?

I'LL BE RIGHT BACK. I'M MAKING A SANDWICH!

Even though cats hate baths and aren't very big fans of water in general, ALL cats CAN swim. In fact, they're very good swimmers.

One breed of cat known as the Turkish Van loves to swim so much that they will jump in water whenever possible.

Tigers are also excellent swimmers. They live in very warm climates, so they tend to swim a lot to keep themselves cool.

If you're ever being chased by a tiger, don't bother jumping in the water. It won't help. Instead, climb a tree. Tigers love to swim, but they're not very good tree climbers.

And if you're ever around the wetlands of Nepal and Myanmar, look for the Fishing Cat. It's a breed of cat with long claws that never fully retract that dives into water to catch fish.

WHAT DID I MISS?

• CHAPTER SIX •

AFTER
THE
BATH

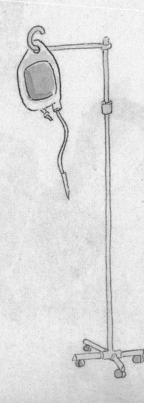

After the bath, Kitty will probably start licking herself quite a bit again. She'll want to be clean in the way she likes to be clean – cat-tongue clean.

This would *NOT* be a good time to pet her.

In fact, Kitty may avoid you altogether for a few hours . . . or days . . . or weeks.

Try not to take it personally. After all, you made Kitty do something that she *HATED* and never wanted to do.

You still did the right thing. Kitty probably won't thank you now. She probably won't thank you EVER. She may even do little things in the next few days to tell you how angry she feels.

BRAND NEW SNEAKER

SOMETHING AWFUL INSIDE

Rinse Kitty off using a hand-held shower attachment if you have one. If not, gently pour water over her as you did earlier.

Again, try not to soak Kitty's head, and use that facecloth to wipe excess soap and water from her face.

Keep rinsing and soaking and wiping Kitty until you're absolutely certain you've removed all of the shampoo.

You may have noticed that Kitty's been making a lot of noise. She's probably trying to tell you something. The following is a list of common cat sounds and their meanings.

 MEOW ⟶ I am hungry.

 MEEE
OOO ⟶ I am very hungry.
WWW?

 MEE   I'm pretty darn
OOW   hungry, and you'd
RRR ⟶   better feed me
OWW   right now or suffer
RRR!   the horrible
              consequences.

2) You both hope you NEVER have to give Kitty a bath again.

• EPILOGUE •

HOW TO GIVE PUPPY A BATH

HEH HEH HEH!

• THE END •

MEOWR
REOWR
YEOWR
HISS
FFT-FFT-FFT
MEOWR.

• GLOSSARY •

Bath • A word you should never say out loud around Kitty.

Combs and wattles •
Fleshy lobes often found on the heads and necks of chickens but rarely found on cats.

Editor • Someone who *brilliantly* supervises the publication of a book like this one *and really deserves most of the credit.*

Esmerelda • The name of Nick Bruel's kitty at home.

Glossary • A list of words and their definitions often found at the back of a book. You have five seconds to find the Glossary for THIS book. Go!

Negotiation • A process that works very well when trying to convince your parents to give you more pocket money, but very poorly when trying to convince Kitty she needs a bath.

Papillae • The hundreds of tiny little hooks on Kitty's tongue that make it feel like sandpaper when she licks your finger.

Plasma • The liquid part of blood. Blood cells float around in it to carry fuel and oxygen around the body. Without plasma, they would be like fish trying to swim without a river. Having some extra plasma around when giving Kitty a bath is useful in case you "lose" a little.

Reverse psychology • A method you can use to get someone to do something by pretending that you want the opposite. But it never works, so don't try it.

Sofa • A soft, comfortable, and very expensive scratching post used by Kitty.

Vegetables • Another word you should probably never say out loud around Kitty.

Vet • An abbreviation of *veterinarian*. A veterinarian is a doctor for animals like Kitty and may be the bravest person on the planet.

GOFISH

NICK BRUEL

What did you want to be when you grew up?
I tell this story all the time when I visit schools. When I was six, there was nothing I liked to do more than to write stories and make little drawings to go with them. I thought the best job in the world was the one held by those people who did the comic strips in the newspapers. What better job is there than to wake up each morning and spend the day writing little stories and making little drawings to go along with them? So, that's what I did. I wrote stories and I drew pictures to go along with them. And I still do that to this day.

When did you realize you wanted to be a writer?
I always liked to write stories. But it wasn't until high school, when I spent a lot of time during summer holidays writing plays for my own amusement, that I began to think this was something I could do as a career.

What's your first childhood memory?
Sitting in my high chair feeling outraged that my parents were eating steak and green beans while all I had was a bowl of indescribable mush.

What's your most embarrassing childhood memory?
Crying my eyes out while curled up in my cubbyhole in my first year at school for reasons I can't remember. I didn't come back out until my mother came in to pick me up from school.

What's your favourite childhood memory?
Waking up early on Christmas morning to see what Santa brought me.

As a young person, who did you look up to most?
My father. He was a kind man with a great sense of humour.

What was your worst subject in school?
True story: when I was thirteen, I was on the reserves for the B-team in baseball. I was asked to bat only twice the entire season. The first time, I got three strikes and was out. The second time, I was beaned in the arm. It was generally recognized that I was the worst player on the team. And since our team lost every single game it played that year, it was decided that I was probably the worst baseball player in all of New York State in 1978.

What was your best subject in school?
Art, with English coming in a close second.

What was your first job?
I spent most of the summer after my third year at university as an arts and crafts director at a camp for kids with visual disabilities in Central Florida. I won't say any more, because I'm likely to write a book about it some day.

How did you celebrate publishing your first book?
I honestly don't remember. A lot was happening at that time.

When *Boing!* came out, I was also preparing to get married. Plus, I was hard at work on *Bad Kitty*.

Where do you write your books?
As I write this, I'm the father of a one-year-old baby. Because of all the attention she needs, I've developed a recent habit, when the babysitter comes by to watch Isabel, of collecting all of my work together and taking it to a nice little Chinese restaurant across the street called A Taste of China. They know me pretty well, and let me sit at one of their tables for hours while I nibble on a lunch special.

Where do you find inspiration for your writing?
Other books. To be productive at what you do, you have to pay attention to what everyone else is doing. I think this is true for writing, for painting, for playing music, for anything that requires any sort of creative output. To put it more simply for my situation . . . if you want to write books, you have to read as many books as you can.

Which of your characters is most like you?
In *Happy Birthday, Bad Kitty,* I introduce a character named Strange Kitty. I can say without any hesitation that Strange Kitty is me as a child. I was definitely the cat who would go to a birthday party and spend the entire time sitting in the corner reading comic books rather than participate in all of the pussycat games.

When you finish a book, who reads it first?
My wife, Carina. Even if I'm on a tight deadline, she'll see it first before I even send it to my editor, Neal Porter. Carina has a fine sense of taste for the work I do. I greatly respect her opinion even when she's a little more honest than I'd like her to be.

Are you a morning person or a night owl?
Both. I suspect that I need less sleep than most people. I'm usually the first one up to make breakfast. And I'm rarely in bed before 11:00 PM. Maybe this is why I'm exhausted all the time.

What's your idea of the best meal ever?
So long as it's Chinese food, I don't care. I just love eating it. If I had to pick a favourite dish, it would be Duck Chow Fun, which I can only find in a few seedy diners in Chinatown.

Which do you like better: cats or dogs?
Oh, I know everyone is going to expect me to say cats, but in all honesty, I love them both.

What do you value most in your friends?
Sense of humour and reliability.

Where do you go for peace and quiet?
I'm the father of a one-year-old. What is this "peez kwiet" thing you speak of?

What makes you laugh out loud?
The Marx Brothers. W. C. Fields. Buster Keaton. And my daughter.

What's your favourite song?
I don't think I have one favourite song, but "If You Want to Sing Out, Sing Out" by Cat Stevens comes to mind.

Who is your favourite fictional character?
The original Captain Marvel. He's the kind of superhero designed for kids who need superheroes. SHAZAM!

What are you most afraid of?
Scorpions. ACK! They're like the creepiest parts of spiders and crabs smashed together into one nasty-looking character. Whose idea was that?

What time of year do you like best?
Spring and summer.

What's your favourite TV show?
I have to mention *The Simpsons*, of course. But I'm very partial to the British mystery series *Lovejoy*.

If you were stranded on a desert island, who would you want for company?
I'm going to defy the implications of that question and say no one. As much as I'm comfortable talking for hours with any number of people, I'm also one of those people who relishes solitude. I've never had any problem with being alone for long periods of time . . . you get a lot more work done that way.

If you could travel in time, where would you go?
America in the 1920s. All my favourite literature, movies, and music comes from that period. I would love to have witnessed or even participated in the artistic movements of that period in history.

What's the best advice you have ever received about writing?
I had a playwriting teacher at university named Bob Butman who gave me superb advice on the subject of writer's block – it's all about PRIDE. It's a complete myth to believe that you can't think about what you want to write next because your mind is a blank. In truth, when you feel "blocked",

it's because you DO have something in mind that you want to put to paper, but you don't feel it's good enough for what you're trying to accomplish. That's the pride part. The best thing, I find, is to put it down anyway and move on. Half the challenge of the writing process is the self-editing process.

What would you do if you ever stopped writing?
I would seriously consider becoming a teacher.

What do you like best about yourself?
I have nice hands. They've always served me well.

What is your worst habit?
Biting other people's toenails.

What do you consider to be your greatest accomplishment?
Adopting our spectacular daughter, Isabel. Actually managing to get my first book (*Boing!*) published comes in second.

Where in the world do you feel most at home?
Home. I'm a homebody. I like to work at home. I like to cook at home. I like to grow my garden vegetables at home. I like being in new and different places, but I dislike the process of getting there. So, because I'm not a big fan of travelling, I just like being at HOME. It's a quality about myself that runs closely with my love of solitude.

What do you wish you could do better?
I wish I was a better artist. I look at the fluidity of line and the luminous colours of paintings by such artists as Ted Lewin, Anik McGrory, Jerry Pinkney and Arthur Rackham with complete awe.

GET READY TO PARTY!

It's Bad Kitty's birthday, and you're invited!

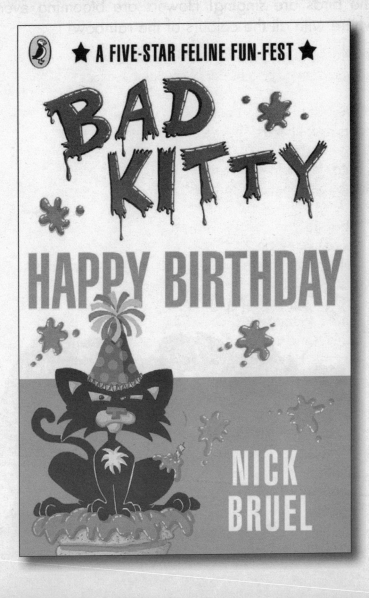

★ A FIVE-STAR FELINE FUN-FEST ★

BAD KITTY

HAPPY BIRTHDAY

NICK BRUEL

GOOD MORNING, KITTY!

Today is going to be a great day! The sun is shining! The birds are singing! Flowers are blooming everywhere with all the colours of the rainbow!

You know what today is, don't you, Kitty? Today is a very special day! Today is the kind of day that only comes once a year! Today is the kind of day that you celebrate ALL day long! Today is the kind of day that deserves a BIG, FUN PARTY!

Now, do you know what today is?

SNORT.

TODAY IS YOUR BIRTHDAY!!!

And that means we start your very special day with a very special **BIRTHDAY BREAKFAST!**

We made all of your favourites . . .

Aardvark **B**agels, **C**lam **D**oughnuts, **E**el **F**ritters, **G**rilled **H**ummingbirds, **I**guana **J**elly, **K**oala **L**emonade, **M**ongoose and **N**uts, **O**rang-utan **P**ancakes, **Q**uail **R**isotto, **S**nake **T**ortillas, **U**nicorn and **V**egetable juice, **W**alrus in **X**O sauce, and for dessert a **Y**ak **Z**abaglione!

Oh, come on, Kitty! You're not going to sleep all day again, are you? All you did yesterday was sleep. All you did the day before yesterday was sleep. And all you did the day before the day before yesterday was sleep.

Are you going to do nothing but sleep every single day?

Will Kitty wake up in time for her party? Or will everyone have fun without her? Find out what happens in **BAD KITTY HAPPY BIRTHDAY**.

SNORE.